A catalogue record for this book is available from the British Library

Published by Ladybird Books Ltd
27 Wrights Lane London W8 5TZ
A Penguin Company
2 4 6 8 10 9 7 5 3

LADYBIRD and the device of a Ladybird are trademarks of Ladybird Books Ltd

© Disney/Pixar MM
Adapted from Walt Disney Pictures' and Pixar Animation Studios' **Toy Story 2**
Mr. Potato Head® is a registered trademark of Hasbro, Inc. Used with permission.
© Hasbro, Inc. All rights reserved. Slinky® Dog © James Industries.

Printed in Italy

The evil Emperor Zurg appeared on the TV screen and shot Buzz Lightyear down.

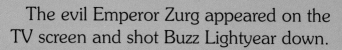 "Oh, no!" Rex moaned. He had lost his favourite Buzz Lightyear video game… again!

The other toys tried to cheer him up – all except Woody. He was too busy getting ready to go to Cowboy Camp with Andy.

But at the last moment, disaster struck! Woody's arm ripped whilst he and Andy were playing with Buzz.

There was no time to repair Woody, so Andy had to leave without him.

Andy's mum put Woody on the mending shelf. There Woody met Wheezy the squeaky penguin, one of Andy's old toys. Just then Andy's mum reached up and took Wheezy from the shelf. She wanted to put him in the yard sale in the garden.

"Goodbye, Woody!" said Wheezy as he disappeared downstairs.

"I'm going to rescue Wheezy!" Woody announced, and he whistled for Buster, Andy's puppy. The two of them ran outside and grabbed Wheezy. But as they headed back for the house, Woody's arm tore again and he tumbled to the ground.

A greedy toy-collector named Al was at the yard sale and when he saw Woody he picked him up and ran to his car. The other toys watched in horror from the window as Al drove off with Woody!

Thinking quickly, Woody used his string as a lasso and pulled Jessie up safely.

At the same moment, Bullseye and Buzz galloped towards them. "Jump! Woody! Jump!" called Buzz.

So, holding Jessie tightly, Woody dropped onto Bullseye's back.

Woody tried to
help Jessie down,
but his weak arm
gave way... "Help!" she
cried, as she fell towards
the wheel.

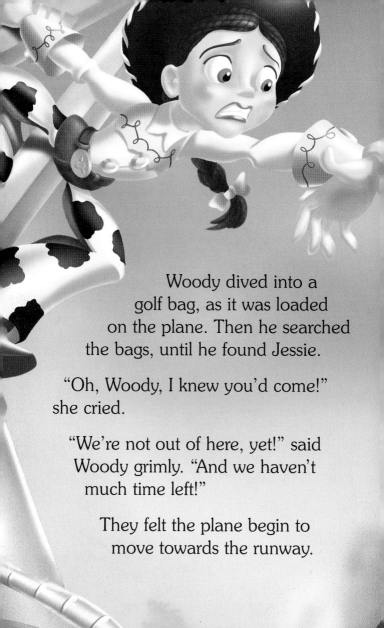

Woody dived into a golf bag, as it was loaded on the plane. Then he searched the bags, until he found Jessie.

"Oh, Woody, I knew you'd come!" she cried.

"We're not out of here, yet!" said Woody grimly. "And we haven't much time left!"

They felt the plane begin to move towards the runway.

"Woody, are you in there!" he called, and he opened the catch.

POW! The Prospector came out fighting. Buzz fought back and quickly packed him in a backpack!

Woody and Bullseye had managed to get out of the suitcase but Jessie was still trapped inside.

"I'm NOT letting Jessie down!" Woody thought. "She deserves another chance to play with a kid who loves her."

Woody, Buzz and Bullseye galloped after Jessie, towards the plane.

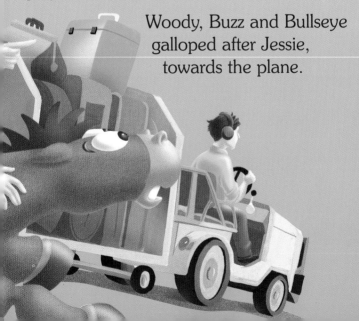

They found him – he was still at the
check-in desk. As Al's suitcase thumped
onto the conveyor belt, the toys jumped
on beside it.

Thousands of boxes, bags and suitcases
swept past them. But Buzz kept his
eyes on Al's green suitcase.

Luckily, Mr Potato Head spotted a pizza truck nearby and the toys jumped in. And so, with Buzz at the steering wheel, Slinky on the pedals, Rex as navigator, and Hamm and Mr Potato Head working the levers, they ziggzagged their way to the airport. There, the toys ran inside, desperately looking for Al.

"We have to get Woody," Buzz shouted. But as they headed for the lift, they heard an evil laugh.

"It's Zurg!" gasped Rex.

Bravely Buzz and the New Buzz fought off the attack. Rex closed his eyes in panic. Then *THWACK!* His tail knocked Zurg off the roof. "I won! I defeated Zurg!" Rex shouted excitedly.

Andy's toys said goodbye to the New Buzz and raced through the hall after Woody.

Andy's toys looked at the New Buzz suspiciously. Then Andy's real Buzz appeared. The toys were confused!

"There's no time to explain," Andy's Buzz said to everyone. "Come on, Woody! Let's go!" But to his amazement, Woody refused. "Yeah!" Woody said sadly. "When I'm worn out, Andy will just throw me away." He turned around and switched on the TV.

Woody watched a small smiling boy on the TV screen. It made him realise just how much he missed Andy. "Hey Buzz! Wait!" he shouted. But Stinky Pete blocked the way.

Buzz turned to help his friend but just then Al came into the room. He scooped his valuable toys into a suitcase and took them to the airport!

Once inside Al's apartment, the New Buzz rushed up to Bullseye. "We're here, Woody!" he yelled.

They stopped outside Al's office. He was on the phone. The toys realised Al was about to take Woody to the airport. They all hid in Al's briefcase as he left the Toy Barn for his apartment.

At that very moment, the real Buzz broke free and raced after Al. But Buzz was being followed… by the evil Emperor Zurg!

Inside the Toy Barn, Buzz looked up at an amazing display of new Buzz Lightyear toys – each one was wearing a super utility pack.

"I could use that!" thought Buzz.

WHAP! His hand was clenched by a new Buzz space ranger. And, before long, Andy's toy was overpowered and imprisoned inside a box on the shelf.

The New Buzz thought Andy's toys were on a mission to defeat the evil Emperor Zurg, so he joined Rex and the others, who were touring the store in a toy sports car.

Not far away, Woody's arm had been repaired. He looked brand new.

"I'm all ready to go home to Andy now!" said Woody.

"I belonged to a little girl once," said Jessie sadly. "She played with me everyday, until she grew up. Then she gave me away. Even the greatest kids outgrow their toys. Listen, Woody, if you stay with us, you'll be remembered for ever."

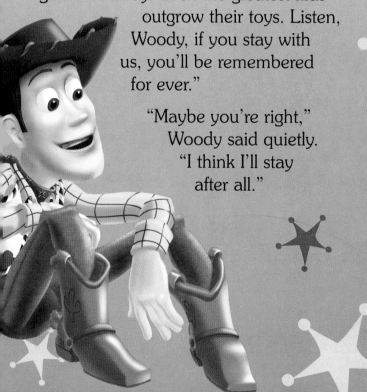

"Maybe you're right," Woody said quietly. "I think I'll stay after all."

The toys each picked up a traffic cone and dashed into the busy road. "Drop!" Buzz yelled and hid beneath his cone. A truck swerved to miss them, spilling its load of concrete pipes. "Go!" cried Buzz.

Mr Potato Head struggled to free his shoe from a piece of bubble gum. He got away seconds before one of the pipes thundered past him.

Ignoring the honking horns and screeching brakes behind them, the toys made it safely inside the Toy Barn.

"Good job, troops!" said Buzz. "Let's split up to look around."

"To Al's Toy Barn… and Beyond!" Buzz shouted bravely. Then he led the way down the street. The five friends walked on through the night. As the sun rose, they came to a busy main road… and spotted Al's Toy Barn.

"We have to get across!" Buzz shouted.

Meanwhile, back at Andy's house, the clever toys had worked out that Al was the owner of the local toy store. That night the toys set out to rescue their friend.

Out on the rooftop, Slinky Dog held on with his paws as, one by one, Rex, Hamm, Mr Potato Head and Buzz used his coils to bungee jump to the ground.

Jessie turned on the TV. Woody was amazed as he watched *Woody's Roundup!* starring Jessie, the yodelling cowgirl, Stinky Pete the prospector doll, Bullseye the horse… and Sheriff Woody!

Woody couldn't believe it. He had once been a television star, and now he was the last piece in a valuable toy collection.

"Al is selling us all to a museum in Japan," explained the old Prospector.

Al took Woody to his apartment and locked him in. Woody looked around for a way to escape but instead he found a floppy little horse called Bullseye and a friendly cowgirl called Jessie.

"Let's show him who he really is!" said an old prospector doll in a box.